The New Kid in Town

Jeff is new in town.

Then . . . the mail came!

For me?

SWiSh!

Who are you?

I am Teeny Genie! I help kids who need me.

Jeff takes his dragon to town.

Too Many Birthdays

With every birthday . . .

. . . Jeff gets older . . .

The Big Game

Go, Jeff, go!

You are out!

Jeff's team wins!

Yay, Jeff!

Thanks a lot, Teeny Genie.

And good luck with the next kid.

Far away, Ann is having a bad day.

I *so* wish you were not my brother!

Story Words

Below is a list of the non-decodable or more challenging words used in this book. To increase your child's vocabulary and reading fluency, review these words with your child before he or she reads the stories.

baseball	genie	teeny
birthday	magic	town
brother	pitcher	throw
dragon	shy	

Sight Words

"Sight words" are words used so frequently that your child should be able to read them without having to phonetically decode them. Below is a list of the non-decodable sight words used in this book.

about	how	now
day	later	old
every	never	started
happy	new	yay